PIGGY'S BATH

David Martin ILLUSTRATED BY Frank Remkiewicz

Introduction

Before your child starts reading, read this story description. Then look through the book together and talk about the pictures.

This story is called *Piggy's Bath.* It's about all the things Piggy gets before he takes a bath, and then what Dad has to get.

Piggy gets a boat.

Piggy gets a duck.

Piggy gets a ball.

Piggy gets a cup.

Piggy gets goggles.

Piggy gets in the bathtub.

Splash!

Dad gets a mop.

HELPING YOUR BRAND-NEW READER

Here's how to make first-time reading easy and fun:

▶ Read the introduction at the beginning of the book aloud. Look through the pictures together so that your child can see what happens in the story before reading the words.

▶ Read one or two pages to your child, placing your finger under each word.

▶ Let your child touch the words and read the rest of the story. Give him or her time to figure out each new word.

▶ If your child gets stuck on a word, you might say, *"Try something. Look at the picture. What would make sense?"*

▶ If your child is still stuck, supply the right word. This will allow him or her to continue to read and enjoy the story. You might say, *"Could this word be 'ball'?"*

▶ Always praise your child. Praise what he or she reads correctly, and praise good tries too.

▶ Give your child lots of chances to read the story again and again. The more your child reads, the more confident he or she will become.

▶ Have fun!

Candlewick Press
99 Dover Street
Somerville, Massachusetts 02144

www.candlewick.com

CANDLEWICK PRESS

0501

Learn more at www.brandnewreaders.com

BRAND NEW READERS

Piggy loves to take baths with lots of toys and LOTS of water.

Includes advice to help you guide and support your brand-new reader.

PIGGY'S BEDTIME

David Martin ILLUSTRATED BY Frank Remkiewicz

Introduction

Before your child starts reading, read this story description. Then look through the book together and talk about the pictures.

This story is called *Piggy's Bedtime.*
It's about the things Piggy and Dad do before Piggy goes to sleep.

Piggy gets in bed.

Dad gets in bed.

Dad reads to Piggy.

Piggy reads to Dad.

Dad kisses Piggy good night.

Piggy kisses Dad good night.

Dad and Piggy smile.

PILLOW FIGHT!

HELPING YOUR BRAND-NEW READER

Here's how to make first-time reading easy and fun:

▶ Read the introduction at the beginning of the book aloud. Look through the pictures together so that your child can see what happens in the story before reading the words.

▶ Read one or two pages to your child, placing your finger under each word.

▶ Let your child touch the words and read the rest of the story. Give him or her time to figure out each new word.

▶ If your child gets stuck on a word, you might say, *"Try something. Look at the picture. What would make sense?"*

▶ If your child is still stuck, supply the right word. This will allow him or her to continue to read and enjoy the story. You might say, *"Could this word be 'ball'?"*

▶ Always praise your child. Praise what he or she reads correctly, and praise good tries too.

▶ Give your child lots of chances to read the story again and again. The more your child reads, the more confident he or she will become.

▶ Have fun!

CANDLEWICK PRESS

0501

Learn more at www.brandnewreaders.com

BRAND NEW READERS®

Piggy's bedtime is a lovely time, but it isn't always quiet.

Includes advice to help you guide and support your brand-new reader.

PIGGY'S PICTURES

David Martin ILLUSTRATED BY Frank Remkiewicz

Introduction

Before your child starts reading, read this story description. Then look through the book together and talk about the pictures.

This story is called *Piggy's Pictures.* It's about how Piggy draws pictures and Dad writes the words to go with the pictures.

Piggy draws a house.

Dad writes "house."

Piggy draws a clown.

Dad writes "clown."

Piggy draws a dinosaur.

Dad writes "dinosaur."

Piggy draws a heart.

Dad writes "Dad loves Piggy."

HELPING YOUR BRAND-NEW READER

Here's how to make first-time reading easy and fun:

▶ Read the introduction at the beginning of the book aloud. Look through the pictures together so that your child can see what happens in the story before reading the words.

▶ Read one or two pages to your child, placing your finger under each word.

▶ Let your child touch the words and read the rest of the story. Give him or her time to figure out each new word.

▶ If your child gets stuck on a word, you might say, *"Try something. Look at the picture. What would make sense?"*

▶ If your child is still stuck, supply the right word. This will allow him or her to continue to read and enjoy the story. You might say, *"Could this word be 'ball'?"*

▶ Always praise your child. Praise what he or she reads correctly, and praise good tries too.

▶ Give your child lots of chances to read the story again and again. The more your child reads, the more confident he or she will become.

▶ Have fun!

Text copyright © 2001 by David Martin
Illustrations copyright © 2001
by Frank Remkiewicz

First edition 2001

ISBN 978-0-7636-1330-3

BNR *Piggy and Dad*

20 21 22 SWT 20 19 18

Printed in Dongguan, Guangdong, China

This book was typeset in Letraset Arta.
The illustrations were done in watercolor and ink.

Candlewick Press
99 Dover Street
Somerville, Massachusetts 02144

www.candlewick.com

CANDLEWICK PRESS

0501

Learn more at www.brandnewreaders.com

BRAND NEW READERS®

Piggy loves to paint pictures. Dad loves Piggy.

Includes advice to help you guide and support your brand-new reader.

PIGGY'S SANDWICH

David Martin ILLUSTRATED BY Frank Remkiewicz

Introduction

Before your child starts reading, read this story description. Then look through the book together and talk about the pictures.

This story is called *Piggy's Sandwich*. It's about how Dad and Piggy make sandwiches for themselves, but then Piggy eats Dad's sandwich too.

Dad makes a sandwich.

Piggy makes a sandwich too.

Dad eats his sandwich.

Piggy eats his sandwich too.

Dad makes another sandwich.

Piggy makes another sandwich too.

Piggy eats his sandwich.

Piggy eats Dad's sandwich too.

HELPING YOUR BRAND-NEW READER

Here's how to make first-time reading easy and fun:

▶ Read the introduction at the beginning of the book aloud. Look through the pictures together so that your child can see what happens in the story before reading the words.

▶ Read one or two pages to your child, placing your finger under each word.

▶ Let your child touch the words and read the rest of the story. Give him or her time to figure out each new word.

▶ If your child gets stuck on a word, you might say, *"Try something. Look at the picture. What would make sense?"*

▶ If your child is still stuck, supply the right word. This will allow him or her to continue to read and enjoy the story. You might say, *"Could this word be 'ball'?"*

▶ Always praise your child. Praise what he or she reads correctly, and praise good tries too.

▶ Give your child lots of chances to read the story again and again. The more your child reads, the more confident he or she will become.

▶ Have fun!

Text copyright © 2001 by David Martin
Illustrations copyright © 2001
by Frank Remkiewicz

All rights reserved.

First edition 2001

ISBN 978-0-7636-1331-0

BNR *Piggy and Dad*

20 21 22 SWT 20 19 18

Printed in Dongguan, Guangdong, China

This book was typeset in Letraset Arta.
The illustrations were done in watercolor and ink.

Candlewick Press
99 Dover Street
Somerville, Massachusetts 02144

www.candlewick.com

CANDLEWICK PRESS

0501

Learn more at www.brandnewreaders.com

BRAND NEW READERS®

When Dad and Piggy make sandwiches, guess who eats more?

Includes advice to help you guide and support your brand-new reader.